A Lot of Otters

BARBARA HELEN BERGER

PHILOMEL BOOKS

To Pat

Copyright © 1997 by Barbara Helen Berger. First board book edition, 2008.
All rights reserved. Published by PHILOMEL BOOKS, a division of
Penguin Young Readers Group. 345 Hudson Street, New York, NY 10014.
Published simultaneously in Canada. Manufactured in China.
L.C. Number: 95-050532
ISBN 978-0-399-25015-6 Special Markets ISBN 978-0-399-25270-9 Not for resale.
10 9 8 7 6 5 4 3 2 1

This Imagination Library edition is published by Penguin Group (USA), a Pearson
company, exclusively for Dolly Parton's Imagination Library, a not-for-profit program
designed to inspire a love of reading and learning, sponsored in part by The Dollywood
Foundation. Penguin's trade editions of this work are available wherever books are sold.

A Lot of Otters

BARBARA HELEN BERGER

PHILOMEL BOOKS

Mother Moon
was looking for her child.
"Where is my moonlet?
Where is—"

Oops.

Mother Moon
was looking for her child.
"Where is my moonlet?
Where is my little one?"

She called and called.
She cried and cried.
With every tear
that fell from her eyes,
a star fell into the sea.

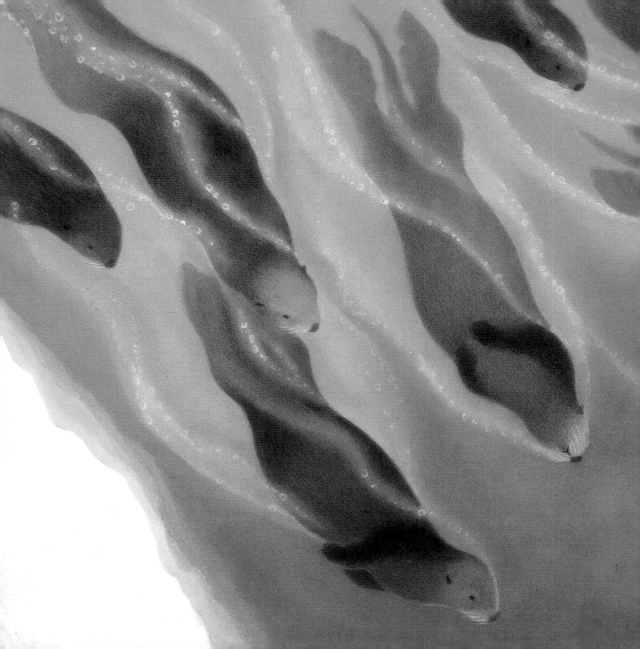

A lot of otters
saw the stars fall.
They dove down
into the dark,

down into the deep.

They carried the stars
up to the top of the sea.

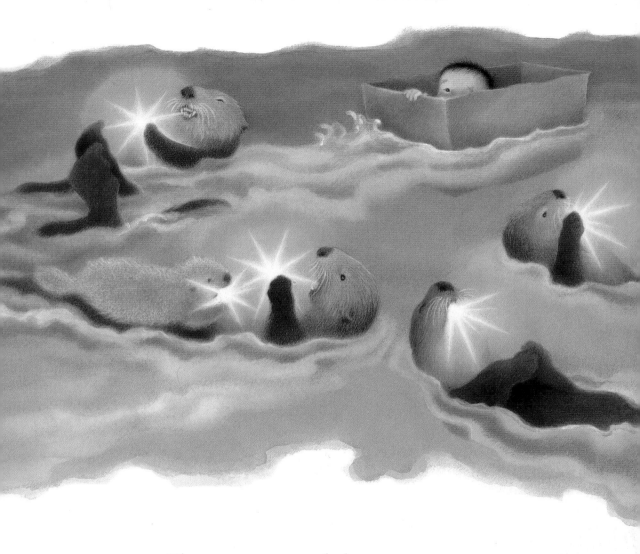

The otters tasted the stars.

They wrestled and rolled
and rubbed the starlight
into their fur.

They bobbed and cavorted
and rollicked around.
They made
such a commotion of light
that Mother Moon
looked down.

"Moonlet? My little one?"
She came running out of the clouds,
over the dark, over the deep.

There
  she found her child,
  safe with a lot of otters

in a sea of stars.